For Kellie

ISBN 978-0-545-61150-3

12 11 10 9 8 7 6 5 4 3 2 1   13 14 15 16 17 18/0

Printed in the U.S.A.   40

This edition first printing, September 2013

Book design by Sara Gillingham
Typeset in Billy
The illustrations in this book were rendered in mixed media.

GOOD NEWS BAD NEWS

Jeff Mack

SCHOLASTIC INC.

Good news!

Bad news.

Good news.

Good news.

Good news.

Bad news.

Bad news.

Good news.

Good news.

Good news.

Bad news!

Very good news.